Henry the Heron

Copyright © 2020

Written by Scott Macdonald
Illustrated by Rebecca Truman

Published by Primal Studios Publishing

First Edition 2020

Every year, when the wind turns cold and the trees start losing their leaves, birds pack their bags and head off on holiday.

Birds of all colours, shapes, and sizes make the journey south.

Meeting up with cousins along the way, they stop off to rest in exotic locations, such as the beautiful Barra.

During their stay on the Isle of Barra, the parents would go to the shops and the children would play at the beach.

The beaches of Barra are wonderful!
With golden sands and blue seas,
the children swoop, dive and splash
having the time of their lives.

As the Barra Summer was
coming to an end, it was
time for the families to
pack up their bags and begin
making their way south from
the cold, towards a hot
island of paradise.

Since there are so many birds
in the sky during this
journey, it can be hard
for mummy and daddy
to see their children.
They are always told
to stay close by.

However, back in Barra,
little Henry the Heron
awakened to find that
everyone had disappeared.

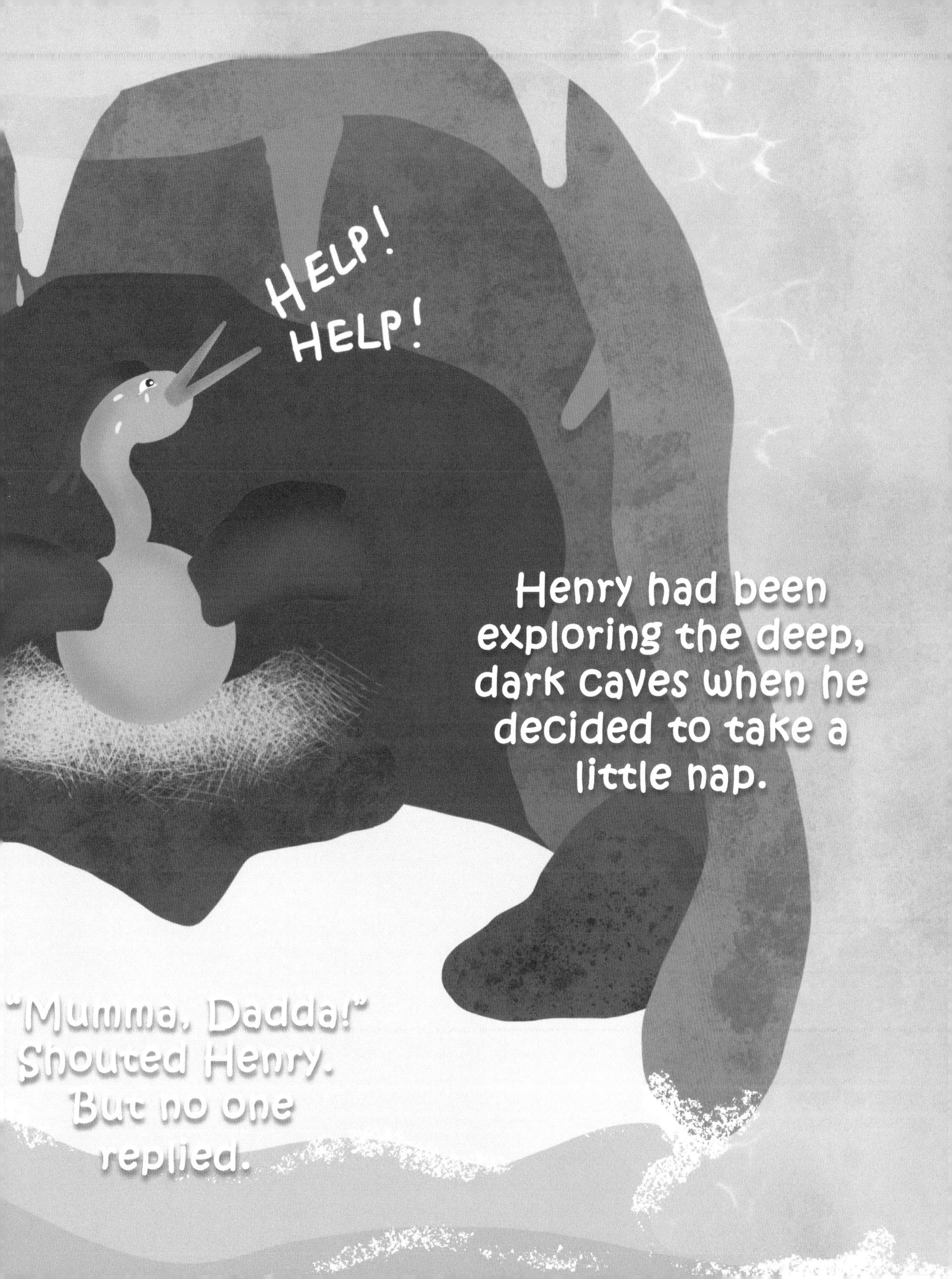

Henry had been exploring the deep, dark caves when he decided to take a little nap.

"Mumma, Dadda!" Shouted Henry. But no one replied.

Then Henry heard a voice. It sounded like it was coming from far in the distance until he looked down and saw a crab.

"What's your name?",asked the crab, to which Henry replied, "My name's Henry, what's yours?".

"I'm Colin, Colin the crab. Well," Colin continued, "you have got yourself in a bit of a pickle! But not to worry, I'll help you find your family."

Henry and Colin made their way back to the beach where Henry last saw his Mummy and Daddy.

When they arrived, they found that a new family of birds had made camp for the night.

Henry had never seen this type of bird before, and they didn't play the same way his brothers and sisters did.

The new family started squawking and dancing, soon Henry and Colin were surrounded by them.

Henry was very scared; however, Colin, although very small, stuck up his arms and started snapping his claws.

The birds flew away, and Colin said "let's go and explore the island. You will be safe with me at your side, Henry."

Henry the Heron was only small, and he hadnt yet mastered using his wings, so off they walked into the village to see if there had been any clues left by Henry's family.

When they arrived in the village, it was a sea of people scurrying around the place, children playing and grown-ups doing their shopping.

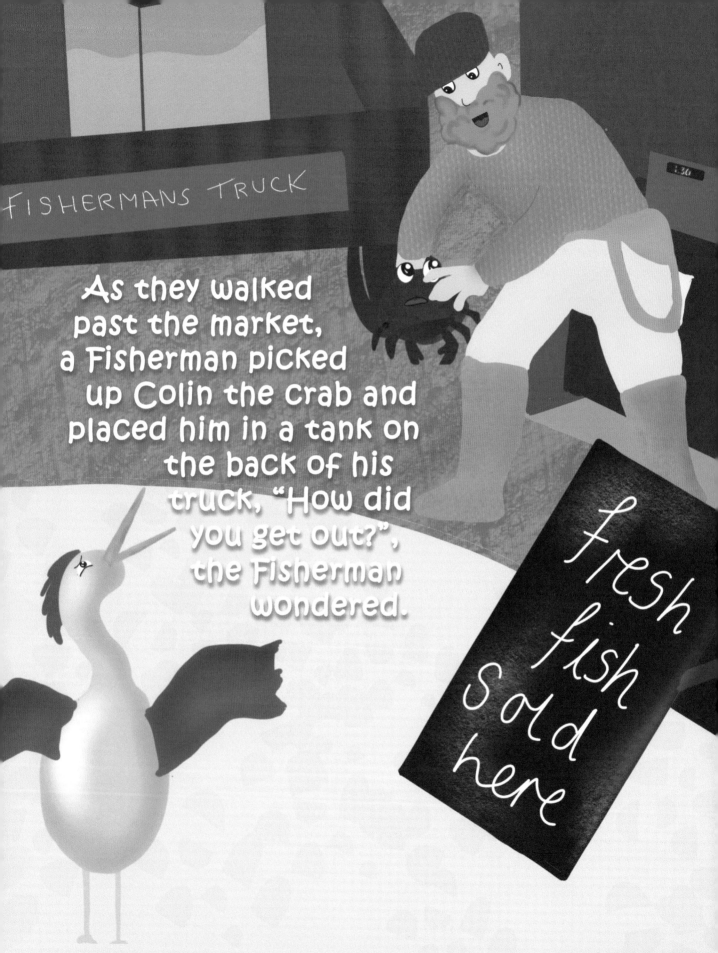

FISHERMANS TRUCK

As they walked past the market, a Fisherman picked up Colin the Crab and placed him in a tank on the back of his truck, "How did you get out?", the Fisherman wondered.

fresh fish sold here

Henry jumped on top of the tank and tried to open the lid, but it was no good.

Colin the crab shouted to Henry the Heron, "Go, run, fly, and find your family before it's too late!"

Henry the Heron stood silent for a few seconds before saying, "NO! You stuck up for me, now it's time for me to stick up for you because that's what friends do for each other!".

Colin the Crab smiled, and with all their might they tried pushing and lifting the lid together.

Just as they managed to lift up the lid, the Fisherman's truck started moving, throwing Henry off the back and onto the road with a big thud, slamming the lid shut again.

Colin the Crab shouted out, "Henry!"
But the truck carried on.

Henry quickly realised
that the only way
to catch up to the
truck would be to
fly.

More determined
than ever, Henry
set himself up and
prepared for take-
off. With his little
legs running faster
than ever before,
he started flapping
his wings, and
before he knew it,
he was in the air on a
rescue mission to save
Colin the crab.

HERMANS TRUCK

Henry saw the truck start to slow down and he knew this was his chance to save Colin, but something else crossed Henry the Heron's mind. Henry had never landed before, not by himself.

So, Henry took a big gulp and aimed for the tank with Colin the Crab inside, and with an almighty crash, Henry the Heron broke through the lid and smashed into the tank.

"Yes, I'm ok!" Henry said, "But we must move quickly!"

"Henry!" Colin shouted with joy, "Are you OK?"

The Fisherman heard the noise and before he could catch Henry and Colin, they were off! Flying higher than Henry had ever been before.

"Have you ever been south for the winter Colin?"
"I had never left my cave before you came along!"
Colin replied.

"Well, how about you come with me?" Henry asked. "There's beautiful sunshine and golden beaches with all the rockpools you could ever dream to explore, and no rain to keep you indoors!"

"You had me at rockpools!" Colin replied. So Henry turned them around and together they started the journey south.

They had been flying for a few days before Colin shouted out, "look over there!"

"Hold on tight, Colin"
They started diving towards the beach, spiralling down faster, and faster, before landing with an almighty crash.

Down on a small beach, on an even smaller island, were a group of birds that looked very familiar.

They made such a clatter when landing it attracted all the birds on the island to them, and they were surrounded once again.

This time though, as Colin was ready to raise his claws, a voice shouted out, "Henry, Henry!" Henry recognised the voice! "Mumma, Mumma!" Called Henry.

Henry and his parents were overcome with emotion as they hugged each other ecstatically.

The rest of the flock started dancing and singing as Henry and his family were reunited, They could now continue the journey south together.

The end.

Printed in Great Britain
by Amazon